PIANOMANIA!

by Manjusha Pawagi   illustrated by Liz Milkau

Liz Milkau

Second
Story
Press

Priya was dying to take piano lessons. That sounds highly unusual, but then Priya was a highly unusual child. She wanted to make the sounds she heard inside her head. The sound of birds and thunder and wind-up toys. Of drums and cannons and choirs of boys. Of waterfalls and marching bands, and even clattering pots and pans.

At first her parents said, "Absolutely not!"

"Remember the painting and ballet lessons you begged for?" asked her mother.

"Remember the aquarium you couldn't live without?" asked her father. And they both shut their eyes to block out the memory of the goldfish Priya forgot to feed.

But Priya did not give up. This was different. She had stopped her art because no one could tell her painting of the family car from her painting of the family cat. She had stopped ballet because she was bored just moving one leg up and down. And, frankly, anyone would get tired of trying to teach goldfish to do tricks. But this time she was serious.

When Priya went to her friends' homes on the weekend, she sat sadly in their kitchens and told their parents that she was not allowed to have piano lessons.

"I can't believe you would let such talent go to waste!" Cole's mother told Priya's mother.

"I wish Hope wanted piano lessons!" Hope's father told Priya's father.

Finally Priya's parents gave in. But they wanted to make sure she would use a piano before they bought one, because pianos cost much more than paintbrushes or goldfish. So they started her off on a cardboard keyboard.

Priya loved it. It was smooth and shiny and had 52 white keys and 36 black keys printed on it. (She knew because she counted them.) It had a big letter C on the middle key so she could always find it with the thumb of her right hand. Best of all, the whole thing folded up neatly to fit in her knapsack. She took it everywhere.

Priya practiced at school and at daycare and at home. Priya's teachers were impressed. Priya's parents were impressed. Priya's little brother was not impressed.

"It doesn't make any sound!" he said.

Priya just smiled at him. Of course it made a sound. It made the most wonderful music she had ever heard. It made the sound of birds and thunder and wind-up toys. Of drums and cannons and choirs of boys. Of waterfalls and marching bands, and even clattering pots and pans.

Priya's parents were so pleased by how much she was practicing that they ordered a real piano, and Priya began taking lessons immediately. She loved the piano's glittering keys and its curly pedals. She loved the little metronome that tick tick ticked so happily.

But there was one problem. Priya did not love the music. Her teacher started her off with songs that had only two notes. It was either C-D-C-D-C-D-C with her right hand, or C-B-C-B-C-B-C with her left hand. Priya wanted to make the sounds she heard in her head. She tried running her fingers up and down the keys. She banged her hands on the high twinkly end, and hit the low rumbling end with her fists.

"Stop that racket!" said her mother.

"Stick to your scales!" said her father.

"I want piano lessons!" said her little brother.

Priya did stop, because she still wasn't making the sounds she wanted to make. "I need reinforcements," she thought. She called all of her friends. She called Cole and Hope. She called Vincent and Jonah and Isabelle. They all came to Priya's house, and they brought their pianos with them. Toy pianos, uprights, and baby grands. Teetering on wagons, gliding on skateboards, and bulging out of knapsacks.

Then, all together, they ran their fingers up and down the keys. They banged their hands on the high twinkly ends, and hit the low rumbling ends with their fists. They stood on their heads and played with their feet. They leapt up high and thumped down on the keys with their bottoms. It was a thousand times louder, but it still did not sound like waterfalls or wind-up toys.

"STOP THAT AWFUL NOISE!" Her parents had to shout to be heard.

Priya stopped, all right. She stopped playing altogether. "The fall recital is coming up," said her mother. "You have to keep practicing," said her father. They did not realize that she was practicing. She was practicing on her cardboard keyboard. It was the only way she could make the sounds she loved, of birds and thunder and wind-up toys. Of drums and cannons and choirs of boys.

Then Priya had another idea. As the concert drew closer, she sent messages to her friends who played other instruments, the ones who played trombones and tubas, cellos and harps.

When the time came for the concert, Priya's parents were nervous, but Priya wasn't nervous at all. When it was her turn, she swept onto the stage just as she had practiced, and she started to play. But she didn't play her recital piece. She ran her fingers up and down the keys. She banged her hands on the high twinkly end, and hit the low rumbling end with her fists. Her mother was aghast. Her father was appalled. Her little brother was asleep. But the rest of the kids were in an uproar. That was the signal!

The children who had already played jumped up and grabbed their instruments again. And the ones who were waiting backstage came running on.

Flutes and violins and recorders pranced around the stage. Trumpets swung from the hanging lights. Cellos and piccolos and bongos wailed and shrieked and pounded. The piano teacher ran around trying to stop the noise. The orchestra conductor tried to help her. But when they grabbed one instrument, the others just got louder.

The commotion went on and on. All the children were loving it. They were giggling and laughing and banging and crashing and screeching.

All except for Priya. She had stopped playing and she was frowning. This didn't sound like the music in her head. Where were the birds and thunder and wind-up toys? The drums and cannons and choirs of boys? The waterfalls and marching bands? Where were the clattering pots and pans?

The piano teacher eventually managed to shoo the children off the stage. The audience slowly filed out.

Priya was left alone at the grand piano. She put her right thumb on middle C and her right pinkie on G. She played three notes, tucked her thumb underneath, and played five more notes slowly in a row. She played the scale faster, and then faster still. She thought she heard the faint sound of a waterfall. With her left hand, she played three notes together in a chord, soft and then loud, and she thought she heard the echo of a cannon.

"Just wait till the spring recital!" she said.

For my little brother Harish, who is now learning to play the piano.
— M.P.

For Mom, Dad and both Steves, with thanks for their encouragement and support.
— L.M.

NATIONAL LIBRARY OF CANADA CATALOGUING IN PUBLICATION DATA

Pawagi, Manjusha, 1967-
Pianomania / by Manjusha Pawagi ; illustrated by Liz Milkau.

ISBN 1-896764-63-0

I. Milkau, Liz II. Title.

PS8581.A8463P52 2003   jC813'.54   C2003-900555-0   PZ7

Edited by Gena Gorrell
Designed by Laura McCurdy

Printed and bound in Hong Kong

Second Story Press gratefully acknowledges the support of the Ontario Arts Council and the Canada Council for the Arts for our publishing program. We acknowledge the financial support of the Government of Canada through the Book Publishing Industry Development Program, and the Government of Ontario through the Ontario Media Development Corporation's Ontario Book Initiative.

Published by
SECOND STORY PRESS
720 Bathurst Street, Suite 301
Toronto, ON
M5S 2R4

www.secondstorypress.on.ca